FR
PA

Parish, Peggy

C2

Granny and the
desperadoes

DATE			
FEB 07			
MAY 2			

Granny and the Desperadoes

But Granny's gun did.
The men saw it.
And then they moved fast.
Soon their hats were
filled with berries.

Granny and the Desperadoes

PEGGY PARISH

ILLUSTRATED BY STEVEN KELLOGG

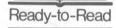

Ready-to-Read

MACMILLAN PUBLISHING CO., INC.
New York
COLLIER MACMILLAN PUBLISHERS
London

for Herb Walker with love

"Huh!" said Granny Guntry.

"The town's all upset.

They say two desperadoes are

prowling around here. Folks want

to stay nights with me because I

won't stay in town. What a lot

of nonsense! I've got nothing they

want. Oh, I smell my pie!"

Granny took her pie out of the oven.

She set it in a window to cool.

Later Granny went to get her pie.

But there was no pie to get.

"Now that's a fine how-de-do,"

she said. "Who took my pie?

Maybe those desperadoes are around!"

Then Granny shook her head.
"No," she said, "they wouldn't
fool with anything like a pie.
It must be the Indians.
Well, I'll soon find out.
Just let me get my gun."
Granny got her gun.
She walked through the woods.
She looked this way and that.

She did not see the pie thieves.

But she did see something else.

"Puddle ducks!" said Granny.

"I want them!"

But Granny shook her head.

"Nope," she said, "I've got to

find that pie first."

And she walked on.

Suddenly she stopped.

She heard low voices.

Granny crept toward the voices.

There sat two men eating her pie.

"Oh, nuts!" said Granny.

"You've eaten it all. And I was
all set for a piece of pie."

"But, mam," said one man,

"we were hungry."

"Are you the desperadoes everybody
is talking about?" asked Granny.

"Oh, no, mam," said the second man.

"We were looking for violets for
Grandma. She does love violets.
And we got lost."

"That's too bad," said Granny.
"But I still want some pie.
And I've no more apples."
Granny stopped and stared.
"Do tell," she said,
"there's a berry patch.
And I do love berry pie.
Now you ate my apples.
So you pick those berries for me.
You can put them in your hats."
The men didn't move.

"I'm Granny Guntry.

Who are you?" asked Granny.

"I'm Hank and he's Jeb,"
one of them said.

"Well, Hank and Jeb," said Granny,

"come along. I'll let you help
me make the pie."
Hank and Jeb walked
in front of Granny.
They went into Granny's house.

"You clean the berries," said Granny,

"I'll make the piecrust."

Soon Granny's mind was all on

her work. Her gun was on the shelf.

Hank nodded to Jeb.

And quietly, quietly, they both got up.

They crept toward the shelf.

They were right behind Granny.

And a board creaked.

Granny turned with a jerk.

The pie dough dropped to the floor.

And Hank and Jeb stepped right in it.

Granny shook her head.

"Now that is a mess," she said.

"Yes, mam, it sure is," said Hank.

"But we'll clean it up."

And they did.

Everybody got back to work.

Finally the pie was made.

"Well, mam, we'll be on our way,"
said Jeb.

"No," said Granny. "Now we'll
catch the ducks."

"Ducks! What ducks?" asked Jeb.

"I saw some puddle ducks,"
said Granny. "I want them."

"Well, mam," said Hank,
"why not just shoot them?"

"That would kill them," said Granny.
"And dead ducks don't lay eggs.
I've a hankering for duck eggs."

"Ducks are hard to catch," said Hank.

"Nonsense," said Granny.

And she told them how to catch ducks.

Soon they were back in the woods.

Hank spread out a big sheet.

He sprinkled corn on it.

"Now call them," said Granny.

"Here ducky, here ducky," called Hank.

He tossed them some corn.

The ducks scrambled after it.

They found the corn on the sheet.

Soon all the ducks were on the sheet.

"Now!" said Granny.

Hank picked up one side of the sheet.

Jeb picked up the other.

And the ducks were caught.

Suddenly there was a loud
crashing sound. Out of the bushes
came a wild hog. It headed
right toward them.
Hank and Jeb scooted up a tree.
And just as the hog reached
the tree, down crashed the limb
they were on. Hank, Jeb and
the limb fell on top of the hog.

"You got him, fellows!" shouted
Granny. "But that's the foolest
way of killing a hog I ever saw."
Hank and Jeb were dazed.
"But I do thank you.

I was wanting some hog meat,"
said Granny.
"You're being mighty good
to an old lady. Now bring
the ducks and the hog along."

At home Granny told Hank and Jeb
what to do with the ducks and hog.
Then Hank said, "It sure looks
like rain. We better get along
toward home, mam."
"Land sakes!" said Granny, "that does
remind me. My roof leaks."
"But, mam," said Hank.

"I'm just a helpless old lady,"
said Granny. "You wouldn't leave
me with a leaky roof, would you?"
Hank and Jeb looked at Granny.
She still held that gun.
"No, mam," said Jeb,
"we wouldn't do that."
So they fixed the roof.
Then Hank nodded to Jeb.
Jeb began talking to Granny.

Hank crept toward Granny's gun.

Suddenly he grabbed it.

Granny turned quickly.

She kicked Hank on the shin.

She kicked with all her might.

Hank stumbled.

He fell against Jeb.

Granny tripped Jeb.

And both men hit the ground.

Granny jerked her clothesline down.

Before they knew what had happened,

Granny had their hands tied.

She picked up her gun.

"Now you two get inside," she said.
Hank and Jeb went.
Granny tied them to chairs.
"You are those desperadoes,
aren't you?" she asked.

"Some folks call us that," said Hank.

"What would your grandma say about that?" said Granny. "You should have stuck with picking violets!"

Hank and Jeb didn't say anything.

"Well, I guess you're ready for your tea anyway," said Granny. "I'll put the kettle on. Then I'll decide what to do with you."

Granny put the kettle on.

Then she sat down to think.

She didn't say anything.

Granny just sat and rocked.

There came a knock at the door.

"My goodness, company!" said Granny.

She opened the door.

"Sheriff!" she said,

"you are a welcome sight.

Come in and have some pie."

"Well, now, that's nice,"

said the sheriff.

"Since I was near here,

I thought I'd pass the time

of day with you.

I'm tired of people telling

me about those desperadoes.

They've probably left

these parts anyway.

Do you think they're around here?"

"Oh, they're around here
all right," said Granny.
"I was just wondering
what to do with them."

"What!" said the sheriff.
He pushed past Granny.
And he saw the desperadoes.
"But how did you do it?"
asked the sheriff.

Granny said, "They wanted to take
my gun. I wouldn't stand for that.
It doesn't shoot. But it's a good gun."
"Doesn't shoot!" said Hank and Jeb.
"Of course not! Did you think it did?
Land sakes! That gun hasn't shot in
years. But it sure is handy.
It reaches high shelves for me.
It brushes spider webs from corners.
No, I couldn't do without my gun."
Hank shook his head.
"It doesn't even shoot," he said.
"All that work for nothing," said Jeb.
"Oh, my, the kettle's boiling,"
said Granny. "I'll make the tea."

And then they all had tea and pie.
When they finished, the sheriff said,
"Well, men, I'll have to take you
with me. I do thank you, mam.
That was mighty good pie."
Hank and Jeb said nothing.

But as they were leaving, Granny said, "Now when the sheriff lets you go and you want to do some honest work, you just come back here. I've got lots that needs to be done."

But when the sheriff let them go,
they headed for distant parts.
Granny never saw Hank or Jeb again.